To Iliana, I hope one day you love your name. –GD

To my dear Abuelita Carmelita. –TM

Reycraft Books
55 Fifth Avenue
New York, NY 10003
Reycraftbooks.com

Reycraft Books is a trade imprint and trademark of Newmark Learning, LLC.

Library of Congress Cataloging-in-Publication Data is available.

ISBN: 978-1-4788-6799-9

Author photo courtesy of Jackie Friedman
Illustrator photo courtesy of Teresa Martinez

Printed in Guangzhou, China
4401/0919/CA21901488
10 9 8 7 6 5 4 3 2 1
First Edition Hardcover published by Reycraft Books

Reycraft Books and Newmark Learning, LLC, support diversity and the First Amendment, and celebrate the right to read.

Dear Abuelo

by GRECIA HUESCA DOMINGUEZ

illustrated by TERESA MARTINEZ

"Abuelo,
I'm going to miss you
so much!" I said.
"And I'm going to miss Mexico too.
But I promise to write
you about

New York."

Dear Abuelo,

I haven't reached New York yet and already
I have so much to tell you! I'm on a plane.
Can you believe it? Mami let me sit in the window seat,
where I can see the tops of the clouds. They are so
fluffy. I imagine walking on them.
Too bad we can't.

Love, Juana

Dear Abuelo,

We live in an apartment now.
We don't have a yard but there is a huge park!
Mami said it's so close, we can walk there.

It's snowing, too. I hope the snow

is so high I can jump in it.

I'll write again soon.

Love, Juana

When I got to my class, my teacher took attendance. She called out "Joanna" ✗ instead of "Juana." ✓ I wanted to say, "My name is Juana," but my mouth wouldn't make a sound.

Dear Abuelo,

I told Mami what happened.
I asked her why I didn't have a name that
was easier to say in English.
And you know what I learned? When
she was little, she wanted
a different name, too!
There were so many girls
named Maria, she
didn't feel like her name was special.
She wanted me to have a special name.
A name that would stand out.

Continued

After dinner, Mami hung Abuela Juana's picture on my wall. She said she wanted me to remember that my name is beautiful, like Abuela.

Guess what? It's hard to be different but I feel proud to have the same name as Abuela.

I got through
my first day of school and will get through
my second day, too!
And I will keep learning English.
Love, Juana

Dear Abuelo,
Guess what?
I made a friend! Her name is
Elizabeth and her family is
from Mexico!
Just like us!!

She was born in the
United States so she
speaks English
and Spanish.

I wish I could speak both.
The teacher told me Elizabeth
would be my class buddy.
I'm so happy!

This is what
she looks like.

Love,
Juana

I told Elizabeth about the teacher pronouncing my name wrong. ☹️ Elizabeth thought I should tell the teacher but I'm too shy.

More on next page →

So Elizabeth

held my hand and we walked right
up to the teacher. Wow!
The teacher seemed as <u>happy</u> as I was
that she could pronounce
my name right. Yay!!

Abrazos,

Dear Abuelo,

I think I'm going to like this school. The other day, the librarian showed me where I could find books in Spanish.

I even found a book by an
author named Juana!
Maybe someday
I'll write a book

in English
and Spanish!

Love,
Juana